The Tiara Club

Butterfly Ball

For Princess Catriona of Trinity,
with much love
VF

www.tiaraclub.co.uk

ORCHARD BOOKS

338 Euston Road, London NW1 3BH

Level 17/207 Kent Street, Sydney, NSW 2000

A Paperback Original

First published in Great Britain in 2007

Text © Vivian French 2007

Illustrations © Orchard Books 2007

The right of Vivian French to be identified as the author of this work has been asserted by her in accordance with the Copyright, Designs and Patents Act, 1988.

A CIP catalogue record for this book is available from the British Library.

ISBN 978 1 84616 470 5

3 5 7 9 10 8 6 4 2

Printed in Great Britain

The paper and board used in this paperback are natural recyclable products made from wood grown in sustainable forests. The manufacturing processes conform to the environmental regulations of the country of origin.

Orchard Books is a division of Hachette Children's Books

www.orchardbooks.co.uk

The Tiara Club

Butterfly Ball

By Vivian French

Illustrated by Sarah Gibb

ORCHARD BOOKS

The Royal Palace Academy
for the Preparation of Perfect Princesses

(Known to our students as "*The Princess Academy*")

OUR SCHOOL MOTTO:
*A Perfect Princess always thinks of others
before herself, and is kind, caring and truthful.*

Ruby Mansions offers a complete education for
Tiara Club princesses with emphasis on the
creative arts. The curriculum includes:

*Innovative Ideas for our
Friendship Festival*

*Ballet for Grace
and Poise*

*Designing Floral
Bouquets
(all thorns will be
removed)*

*A visit to the Diamond
Exhibition
(on the joyous occasion of
Queen Fabiola's birthday)*

Our headteacher, Queen Fabiola, is present at all times,
and students are well looked after by the head fairy
godmother, Fairy G, and her assistant, Fairy Angora.

Our resident staff and visiting experts include:

*KING BERNARDO IV
(Ruby Mansions Governor)*

*LADY HARRIS
(Secretary to Queen Fabiola)*

*LADY ARAMINTA
(Princess Academy Matron)*

*QUEEN MOTHER MATILDA
(Etiquette, Posture and
Flower Arranging)*

We award tiara points to encourage our Tiara Club princesses towards the next level. All princesses who win enough points at Ruby Mansions will attend a celebration ball, where they will be presented with their Ruby Sashes.

Ruby Sash Tiara Club princesses are invited to go on to Pearl Palace, our very special residence for Perfect Princesses, where they may continue their education at a higher level.

PLEASE NOTE:
Princesses are expected to arrive at
the Academy with a *minimum* of:

TWENTY BALLGOWNS
(with all necessary hoops,
petticoats, etc)

TWELVE DAY DRESSES

SEVEN GOWNS
suitable for garden parties,
and other special
day occasions

TWELVE TIARAS

DANCING SHOES
five pairs

VELVET SLIPPERS
three pairs

RIDING BOOTS
two pairs

Cloaks, muffs, stoles, gloves
and other essential
accessories as required

Hello - I'm Princess Amy - and
it's SO lovely that you're here at
Ruby Mansions. Do you know the others
who share Poppy Room? Chloe and Georgia
and Olivia and Lauren and Jessica? I do
hope so, because they're really, really lovely.
We were HUGELY excited when we heard
that we were going on summer camp to
study butterflies. Even knowing horrible
Diamonde and Gruella would be there
as well didn't stop us talking
non-stop while we packed...

Chapter One

Have you ever been away on a weekend school trip? Getting ready took AGES! Fairy G (she's our school fairy godmother, and she looks after us) kept appearing in Poppy Room with more and more and MORE instructions. Just as I tied up the top of my backpack for about the twentieth

time she popped her head round
the door and said, "Did I remind
you to wear sensible shoes?"

"Yes, Fairy G!" we chorused.

"And to bring waterproofs in case it rains?"

"YES, Fairy G!"

"Good." Fairy G beamed at us.

"Then I think that's everything. See you downstairs in five minutes!"

Jessica collapsed on her bed with a loud sigh. "I'm worn out already, and we haven't even got there," she said.

"It's going to be fun, though." Olivia swung her backpack over her shoulder. "Wow! This is heavy!"

"Do you think we'll be sharing the same room at Butterfly Lodge?" Lauren asked.

Chloe looked shocked. "I should hope so!" she said. "I don't want to have to share with Diamonde and Gruella!"

Georgia giggled. "I shouldn't think they'd be very pleased if they found they were sharing with you, actually – you know what they're like."

I looked at the clock on the wall.

"Hey – we'd better go! Hurrah! Off to Butterfly Lodge!" And we picked up our backpacks and hurried down the stairs.

We were just crossing the hall when we met Diamonde and Gruella skipping towards the door. Behind them two page boys

were struggling to carry two enormous suitcases.

"Ooooh," Diamonde sneered as she stopped to stare at us. "Look, Gruella! You'd never ever know they were princesses, would you? They look like servants carrying those big bags!"

"They're backpacks," I said. "And why aren't you carrying yours? Queen Fabiola says it's good for us to be independent."

"Mummy says we ALWAYS have to remember that WE are very special," Gruella told me. "She would NEVER allow us to carry our luggage like ORDINARY people."

"But Perfect Princesses mustn't expect to be treated differently," I said indignantly. "It's like Queen Fabiola told us at the beginning of term – 'a Perfect Princess must treat everyone they meet with consideration and respect'."

"Pooh!" Diamonde turned up her nose. "Listen to know-it-all Amy! I suppose YOU'D respect a washerwoman!"

"Amy would probably offer to carry her bags of smelly washing," Gruella tittered.

I couldn't help it. I lost my temper. "Yes I would!" I snapped. "Just because I wear a tiara doesn't make me better than anyone else! And if you think YOU'RE better it only goes to prove you AREN'T!" And I swung away across the hall and threw myself into the nearest coach.

The rest of Poppy Room were already sitting inside. I pulled the door shut as I got in.

"Phew!" Lauren said. "That really told Diamonde!"

I was beginning to simmer down a bit. "Sorry," I said. "But she's SO horrible. They both are."

And at that exact moment I saw Diamonde and Gruella standing RIGHT outside, and they both looked absolutely furious.

"Oops," I whispered to Chloe as the twins stamped away. "Do you think they heard me?"

Chloe smiled at me. "Don't worry about it. We're going to have a fabulous weekend chasing butterflies. We probably won't even see them that much!"

Queen Fabiola (she's our lovely headteacher) had given us a long lecture about Butterfly Lodge. She told us it used to be an old hunting lodge belonging to King Heber of Harringley, but because he didn't believe in hunting he'd turned it into a wonderful centre for rare butterflies. Queen Fabiola said the king had planted all kinds of special plants and flowers for the caterpillars, and he'd also built a totally amazing glasshouse where he bred the very rarest kind of butterflies.

It sounded SO exciting – but the most exciting thing of all was our special project! Not only were we supposed to make notes about the life history of the butterfly and stuff like that, but we had to make drawings of our favourites and choose EXACTLY the right colours to paint them in. Why?

Because there was going to be the most glorious Butterfly Ball at

Ruby Mansions. And Queen Fabiola said we could design our very own dresses in the colours of our favourite butterflies, and she would have them made for us! And the most wonderful thing of all was that Fairy G had promised a very VERY special prize for the princesses who designed the best dresses...they would float down to the Butterfly Ball on a magical flower petal carpet!

So you can understand why we just couldn't WAIT to get to Butterfly Lodge. At first we kept looking out of the coach windows to see if we were there yet, but after a while it got boring.

"How long did Fairy G say the journey would be?" Lauren asked as we went up yet another hill.

"I don't think she did," Jessica said. "She said something about arriving in time for supper, though."

"SUPPER?" Olivia sat bolt upright. "But it's only the middle of the afternoon!"

"I'm going to go to sleep," Georgia said, and she snuggled up against my shoulder. "Wake me when we arrive."

"Good idea," I said, and I yawned...and before long we were all fast asleep.

We were woken by the sound of voices, and as we stretched and opened our eyes we realised the coach had stopped. A moment later Fairy G tapped on the window. "Hurry up, my dears! We're here! And King Heber is waiting to welcome you."

We grabbed our backpacks and tumbled out of the coach. A fat little king was standing on the stone steps of what looked like an ordinary castle that had somehow shrunk. There was a moat, and a drawbridge, and an iron-studded front door, and the roof was a mass of towers and turrets – but it was TINY! I couldn't help staring.

The little king saw me and frowned. "No gawping, girl! You may think you're too grand for a nifty little place like mine, but I can assure you that Butterfly Lodge is a splendid place. Splendid!"

I tried my best to curtsey, although it's really hard when you're wearing a heavy backpack. "Please, please excuse me, Your Majesty," I said. "I was looking at the towers." The king didn't look very impressed, so I hastily added,

"And I'm very grateful that you have allowed us to visit your beautiful butterflies."

King Heber almost smiled. "Good! Good! Glad to hear it. Now, come inside. Quickly, now!" And he hustled us in the door.

As we walked into the hallway I saw Diamonde, dragging her enormous suitcase behind her. She glared at me as if it was my fault she didn't have someone to carry it. "Don't think I didn't hear what you said about us," she hissed. "We're going to get you for that!"

Chloe grabbed my arm. "Ignore her," she whispered. "This way – Lauren's found our room." And she hurried me away before I could say anything.

Chapter Three

We were VERY pleased to discover we were all in the same room, although it was so small we had to take turns unpacking our backpacks. We had bunk beds with the cosiest looking sleeping bags – and our pillows were soft and very fluffy!

"Do you think Diamonde and

Gruella have bunk beds?" Olivia asked.

"They've probably told King Heber that Mummy will only let them sleep in a four-poster," Jessica said with a giggle.

Chloe shook her head. "You can't help feeling sorry for them sometimes. It does sound as if their mother is pretty awful."

"That's right," Georgia agreed. "Most of the time they're just repeating what she's told them."

I suddenly remembered how I'd snapped at Diamonde, and I began to feel guilty. Maybe, I told myself, maybe I'd tell her I was sorry I'd got so angry. After all, Perfect Princesses are always kind and caring...

"Wake up, Amy!" Jessica snapped her fingers under my nose. "Didn't you hear Fairy G bellowing at us from downstairs? It's supper time!"

I didn't have a chance to say anything to Diamonde and Gruella during supper because King Heber spent the WHOLE TIME telling us about his butterflies!

My friends and I could hardly keep our eyes open, even though we'd slept in the coach. We were really glad when we were allowed to stagger off to bed.

I don't know if it was because we'd had that long sleep in the coach or what, but I woke up REALLY early the next morning, The sun was beaming into our room, and the sky was bright blue. My friends were still fast asleep, and even though I opened the window wide they didn't stir.

"I'll go and have a look outside," I thought. King Heber had told us we could go anywhere we liked just as long as we NEVER opened the door to the glasshouse, and I thought it would be fun to have a look round. I crept out of our room and down the stairs, and found Fairy G sitting in a chair in the hall. She did look funny. Everything in King Heber's lodge was so small, and Fairy G is so big – I couldn't help wondering if she'd ever get out of the chair again.

"Good morning, Amy!" she bellowed cheerfully. "I'm waiting for my coach. Fairy Angora's coming from Silver Towers to look after you today, and I'm

going back to Ruby Mansions.
Just off for a walk, are you?"

"Yes, Fairy G," I said. "Is that
all right?"

Fairy G beamed at me. "Of course! Have you got your sketchbook and paints? Don't forget you're studying butterflies!"

"Oh!" I'd forgotten. "I'll go and get them!" And I turned and zoomed back up the stairs. Halfway up I met Diamonde and Gruella, and they glared at me.

"Been out already, have you?" Diamonde sneered. "I suppose YOU were trying to find the best butterfly by sneaking out early."

I was about to say I certainly wasn't doing any such thing, when I remembered I was supposed to be Kind and Caring.

"I haven't been out yet," I said. "I forgot my sketchbook. And—" I took a deep breath, and smiled in as friendly a way as I could manage, "I'm really sorry if I was snappy yesterday."

Gruella began to smile back at me, but Diamonde gave her a sharp push. "It's no good trying to be friends with us now. We're not going to help you draw any butterflies – so there!" And she stormed past me, pulling Gruella behind her.

"Oh well," I thought as I went to fetch my sketchbook. "I did try."

Chapter Four

When I got back to our room my friends were awake at last.

"Hang on a minute," Chloe said, "and we'll come out with you."

I sat on the edge of my bed and waited for the others to get dressed. They were just about ready when there was the weirdest noise from downstairs – it sounded like someone beating the most enormous gong.

"Do you think that means breakfast is ready?" Georgia asked.

"I don't know," I said. "Isn't it still a bit early?"

"Maybe we'd better go and see," Jessica suggested. "It might be a fire alarm or something like that."

We joined the stream of other princesses who were rushing downstairs to see what was going on, and ran into the hall. The noise was coming from the room where we'd had supper, so we hurried

inside – and there was King Heber
banging an old metal bowl as hard
as he could. Fairy Angora was
standing beside him looking
anxious, and the twins were sitting
at one of the tables looking SO
pleased with themselves.

As soon as we were all in the dining room King Heber stopped. "Something TERRIBLE has just happened here!" he announced. "Somebody left the door of my glasshouse open, and one of my Clouded Yellow butterflies has flown out! I don't know who could have been so irresponsible,

but I am VERY angry...and VERY disappointed." He pulled out a large purple handkerchief and wiped his face. "If these two sensible girls hadn't come running to tell me that the door was open, who KNOWS what might have happened?"

Diamonde put her hand up.

"Yes, my dear?" King Heber peered at her. "What is it?"

Diamonde fluttered her long eyelashes, and looked down as if she was shy.

"If you please, Your Majesty, I just wanted to say that I do know there was one princess who was out in the garden very early this morning. Of course I can't say who it was, because that would be sneaky..."

King Heber patted her shoulder. "Good girl! Good girl! Can't bear sneakiness."

Diamonde looked very, very disappointed, but Gruella called

out, "It was Amy! SHE was up earlier than anyone! We saw her coming in from the garden AGES ago!"

And absolutely EVERYONE turned to stare at me, and of course I couldn't help blushing the most terrible fiery red.

"Amy – is this true?" Fairy Angora was looking at me in surprise.

"Please, Fairy Angora, I only got as far as the door," I explained. "I was going to go out, but I met Fairy G and she reminded me I hadn't got my sketchbook and paints, so I went back to fetch them."

I'd expected Fairy Angora to nod, and tell me everything was all right – but she didn't. She gave a little gasp, and said, "But Amy, angel – you couldn't have seen Fairy G! She went back to Ruby Mansions late last night.

I've just unpacked my things in her room, and the bed's not been slept in."

I could feel my mouth dropping wide open. "B–b–but she said she was waiting for her coach—" I stuttered.

Fairy Angora shook her head sadly. "I'm sorry, Amy dear. There was no Fairy G here when I came."

"See?" Diamonde pulled at King Heber's sleeve. "She's the one! SHE let the butterfly out!"

And to my absolute horror I heard the king say, "I'm afraid you're right, my dear. The evidence does seem to be stacked against Princess Amy." He folded his arms, and looked at me coldly. "There's only one thing to be done. I must ask you to leave Butterfly Lodge just as soon as a carriage can be made ready. Please return to your room until you are called."

Chapter Five

Can you imagine how I felt as I trailed out of the dining room? I could feel every single pair of eyes staring at me, and I wanted the floor to open up and swallow me. And although I knew I hadn't left the lodge, I started to wonder – had I really seen Fairy G? But as I hauled myself up the staircase

I knew nobody could have imagined Fairy G bulging out of the chair in the hall. She must have been real! I heaved a huge sigh as I wished and WISHED she was still at the lodge.

Once I reached my room, I packed my things as quickly as I could. Then I sat down on my bunk bed and stared miserably round. What would happen to me now? Would I still be allowed to go to the Butterfly Ball? I didn't have any pictures, so I wouldn't have a dress... I sniffed hard, and wiped away a tear.

And then I saw it!

A bright yellow butterfly was gently opening and closing its wings in the corner of our room...

I could hardly breathe, I was so excited. Very VERY gently I shut the window, and very VERY slowly I moved towards the butterfly. There was a glass on the window sill, and I picked it up together with my sketchbook, and I CREPT forward...

KNOCK KNOCK!

There was a loud bang on the door, and the butterfly flipped its wings and flew across to the opposite corner. I waited for it to settle again, and then I opened the door just a crack. Chloe was standing outside, with Jessica, Georgia, Lauren and Olivia.

"King Heber says your coach is here," Chloe said. "Oh, Amy – we KNOW you didn't do it—"

"Sssh!" I said. "One of you go and get King Heber! Quick!

I've found the butterfly!"

"Wow!" Jessica's eyes opened wide, and she turned and absolutely ZOOMED down the stairs.

A second later the king puffed
up, a butterfly net in his hand.

"Is it really here?" he asked. "WHERE? Are you sure it's the Clouded Yellow?"

I pointed to the butterfly, and with one swoop of his net King Heber caught it. He inspected it carefully, and then smiled SUCH a huge smile we couldn't help smiling back. "Well done, young lady!" he said, and he shook my hand so hard it hurt. "Well DONE! Now, I'll get this into my glasshouse. When we've bred a dozen or so little caterpillars I'll send it back into the wild... Oh, Princess Amy! I can't tell you how pleased I am to find it again!"

"Please, Your Majesty," Olivia said, "does that mean Amy doesn't have to go back to Ruby Mansions?"

King Heber stopped, and scratched his head. "H'm," he said.

"There's a question..." Then he laughed, and gave a little skip. "I say she can stay. After all, I've got my butterfly! I'll give you a task to do instead, Amy. Come with me!"

I felt a million zillion times better going down the staircase behind King Heber. He marched me across the hall and out into the garden, where lots of princesses were wandering about looking at the butterflies fluttering over the flowers.

"You can help me put the Clouded Yellow back," the king said. "And I'll show you how to feed the butterflies."

We went on along a little twisty path, and at the end came to a tall glass door.

"Just open it, will you?" the king said. "I don't want to let this chap go before we're safe inside."

"Erm..." I said, looking at the glass. "There doesn't seem to be a handle..."

"What?" King Heber stopped dead, and stared at me. "What did you just say?"

"I can't see a handle," I repeated.

"WE'LL show you how to open it!" Diamonde and Gruella suddenly appeared beside us, as if by magic.

Diamonde simpered at King Heber. "How VERY kind of you to forgive naughty Amy."

"Look!" Gruella pointed to a tiny handle way up at the edge of the glass. "THAT's where you open it! It took us AGES to discover..." Her voice died away.

King Heber didn't say anything for a moment. Then he opened the door, carefully let the yellow butterfly go, and closed the door again. "Amy, my dear," he said as he took my arm. "I owe you a big apology. I hope you will accept it."

"Of course!" I said. "But please, could I still help you feed the butterflies? And would it be all right if my friends helped too?"

Chapter Six

And that's why it wasn't me that went back to Ruby Mansions in the coach, but Diamonde and Gruella. And my friends and I dripped the sugar water into the butterflies' feeding dishes, and the butterflies were SO beautiful as they fluttered down to sip at it...and we painted MASSES of pictures! Of course Georgia's were the best (she's FABULOUS at painting) but King Heber said he liked my picture of the Clouded Yellow very much indeed. I was THRILLED!

On the Sunday Queen Fabiola came rolling up in a carriage to inspect our work, and Fairy G came with her. I'd almost forgotten about the horrible mistake King Heber had made the day before, but while we were having our lunch Lauren suddenly said, "Fairy G, WHEN did you go back to Ruby Mansions? Amy said she saw you yesterday morning."

Fairy G nodded. "So she did!"

Fairy Angora looked puzzled. "But you can't have. I arrived ever so early from Silver Towers, and you hadn't slept in your room.

The bed was all made up with clean sheets..."

Fairy G laughed her great big booming laugh. "Fairy Angora! Haven't you ever heard of MAGIC? I haven't made a bed myself for years and years and YEARS!"

"Oh!" Fairy Angora's cheeks went very pink. "Of COURSE! How silly of me!"

"Ahem!" Queen Fabiola coughed loudly. "Fairy G, don't you think we should announce the winners of the dress designing competition?"

"I certainly do." And Fairy G

waved her wand, so that tiny
sparkles of light danced in the air
around us...and came twinkling
down on our hair.

Chloe, Jessica, Olivia, Georgia, Lauren and I suddenly felt this EXTRAORDINARY feeling ...

and we actually floated up in the air for a second before coming back down into our seats with a bump!

"There! There's some MORE magic for you!" Fairy G said cheerfully. "And I can tell you that only the very BEST students react to fairy dust like that...so guess who will be floating down to the Butterfly Ball on a magical poppy petal carpet?"

My friends and I stared at each other, our eyes shining.

"Us?" I whispered.

Fairy G nodded. "That's right. Poppy Room!"

And as Queen Fabiola and King Heber and all the other princesses clapped and clapped and CLAPPED we gazed at each other in wonder.

We were going to go to the Butterfly Ball – and we were going to FLOAT there on a magical carpet!

Oooh – don't you just LOVE parties?
And the Butterfly Ball is going to be
SO special – I can't wait! And all the
very nicest people will be there. Chloe,
Amy, Georgia, Lauren and Jessica from
Poppy Room – and YOU! We'll have
such fun – just as long as the horrible
twins don't get in the way.
Whoops! I'm so excited I almost
forgot to tell you who I am. I'm
Princess Olivia, and I'm so glad
you're in the Tiara Club with me!

Chapter One

"SH!" Georgia said, and yawned. "Go to SLEEP, Olivia!"

But I couldn't. I was lying in bed in Poppy Room, and we'd all been talking about the Butterfly Ball before Fairy G (she's the Princess Academy fairy godmother) came to say goodnight. Georgia and Amy and I had gone on talking after the main light was turned off, even though we were SO not meant to. I was still trying to decide what colour dress to have.

"Georgia," I said, "I think I'm going to choose purple after all...not orange."

But Georgia didn't answer. She was fast asleep. I sighed, and turned over. "Amy...are you awake?" I asked. "Don't you think purple will be the nicest?"

"I think you'll look fabulous," Amy said sleepily. "Now go to sleep..."

I smiled, and shut my eyes – but it was no good. All kinds of different colours whizzed about in my brain, and I felt SO wide-awake.

Then I heard a sound...a sort of scuffling outside our room. And the door opened VERY quietly...

I sat bolt upright. I wasn't exactly scared, because I thought it was probably Fairy G checking we were asleep, but my heart was thumping. I held my breath and listened very carefully. There was another little scuffle, and this time it sounded as if it was actually inside Poppy Room.

"Who's there?" I asked as bravely as I could.

There was a sudden rustle, and a thump, and the door closed.

"Amy! Georgia! Anyone!" I hissed. "Did you hear that?"

There was no answer. I pulled back my covers, and tiptoed across the room. I was almost sure I could still hear noises, so I took a deep breath, and opened the door just a little – and gasped!

Diamonde and Gruella were creeping away along the dimly lit corridor towards the stairs. A second later, they were gone.

I didn't know WHAT to do. Diamonde and Gruella had both been behaving in the strangest fashion ever since we came back from Butterfly Lodge, where they'd got into dreadful trouble for being horrible to Amy.

Our headteacher, Queen Fabiola, had given them SUCH a telling-off, and they'd been given loads of minus tiara points. They'd even been told they might not be allowed to attend the Butterfly Ball, but they'd cried their eyes out and PROMISED to be good, and Queen Fabiola took pity on them. And they really did seem much better – but somehow it didn't feel quite right. Even when they were helping tidy up the classroom, or telling someone how lovely they looked, they kept giving each other sneaky little smiles. It seemed to be only me that noticed, though.

I'd asked my friends if they thought the twins were up to something and they'd shaken their heads.

"I think they really are trying to be good," Amy said.

"That's right," Jessica agreed, and Lauren, Chloe and Georgia nodded.

*

I stood in the doorway, and thought about what I'd seen. At last I decided I'd tell my friends in the morning, and see what they said. I was just about to go back to bed when Fairy G came thumping along the corridor in the other direction.

"OLIVIA!" she boomed. "What ARE you doing? You've got SUCH a busy day tomorrow. The Grand High Duchess Delia is coming with her assistants to start making your dresses, so I want you bright-eyed and ready to help. Back into bed AT ONCE!"

"Yes, Fairy G," I said. For a moment I wondered if I should tell her about Diamonde and Gruella, but Perfect Princesses NEVER tell tales. I hurried back to bed, and snuggled into my pillow. "Yes, I thought dreamily. "I'll have a purple dress like that beautiful Purple Emperor butterfly... or violet. Very pale, and sort of shimmery..."

Chapter Two

The next thing I knew Lauren was shaking me awake. "Come ON, Olivia!" she said. "You've only got ten minutes before the breakfast bell!"

I absolutely ZOOMED out of bed, and scrambled into my clothes as fast as I could. Even so I was only just sitting down for

breakfast when our headteacher,
Queen Fabiola, came hurrying in.
Her hair was standing up on end,
and she looked flustered.

"LATE, Princess Olivia?" she said. "I hope this doesn't mean you don't appreciate what a special day this is!"

I could feel myself blushing as I made my best curtsey. "I'm so sorry, Your Majesty."

"What? What's that you say?" Queen Fabiola frowned, and stomped on past me.

I heard Diamonde and Gruella snigger, and then I suddenly remembered what I'd seen the night before. I grabbed Chloe's arm, and said, "Hey! Guess what—" but I was interrupted. Queen Fabiola was standing in the middle of the dining hall with her hand up for silence.

"Good morning, princesses!" she said. "Now, my first duty is to welcome the Grand High Duchess Delia, who is going to be helping you with your dresses for the Butterfly Ball. As soon as you've finished your breakfast I'd like you to make your way to the sewing room upstairs. Secondly—" Queen Fabiola suddenly looked anxious. "I seem to have misplaced my ear trumpet. Has anyone noticed it lying around somewhere?"

Queen Fabiola stopped, and there was a silence. Nobody put

up their hand. Our headteacher sighed. "I'm quite sure none of my Perfect Princesses would hide it away on purpose. That would be a very unkind trick to play. If anyone does find it, do PLEASE bring it straight to me."

As Queen Fabiola moved away I caught sight of Diamonde. She was digging Gruella in the ribs with her elbow and pointing at Amy, and there was SUCH a nasty look on her face. The moment she saw me looking she smiled sweetly and began to clear up the breakfast plates.

"Dear Olivia," she cooed. "You must be SO looking forward to making your beautiful dress. You'll look LOVELY in purple. Won't she, Gruella?"

"Oh YES," Gruella agreed. "Much nicer than in orange. May I pass you the toast?"

I thanked Gruella, but my brain was buzzing. How did the twins know I'd decided to have a purple dress? They must have heard me talking to Georgia the night before, when they were tiptoeing about outside our room. Then I thought, maybe they came INTO our room? And I had an idea...

"Excuse me a moment," I said, and I jumped up from the breakfast table. "I'll see you all in the sewing room!"

I could see my friends looking astonished, but I didn't have time to explain. I zoomed up to Poppy Room as fast as I could. I whizzed inside, and peered round.

And then I saw it. Queen Fabiola's ear trumpet. It was under Amy's bed.

"I KNEW it!" I said out loud, and I snatched up the trumpet in triumph.

Chapter Three

I bounced down the stairs feeling really pleased with myself. I'd just reached the bottom when I saw Queen Fabiola and Fairy G coming towards me, and I held out the ear trumpet. "I've found it, Your Majesty!"

"Well done, Princess Olivia!" my headteacher beamed at me.

"Was it on the stairs?"

"Oh NO, Your Majesty," I said cheerfully. "It was under Amy's bed."

And then I realised how truly
DREADFUL that must sound!
I blushed and began to stutter.
"I didn't mean…that is…I mean…
of course it was NOTHING to do
with Amy. She'd NEVER do
anything like that—" I could feel
myself getting into more and more
of a muddle.

Queen Fabiola gave me a stern
look. "Princess Olivia, will you
please tell me how my ear trumpet
came to be in Poppy Room?"

My mouth opened and shut
several times, but no words came
out. I didn't know what to say.
I couldn't tell tales – and besides,

I couldn't be ABSOLUTELY certain it had been the twins. I hadn't actually seen them hiding the trumpet under Amy's bed.

"If you please, Your Majesty," I said at last, "I don't know how it got there. But I do know it wasn't anything to do with Amy."

Fairy G stepped forward and took the ear trumpet out of my hands. "I think we'd better send you up to the sewing room," she boomed, and she turned to Queen Fabiola. "There does indeed seem to be a mystery here, Your Majesty, but perhaps you'd be kind enough to let me deal with it?"

The queen nodded, but she didn't look pleased. "I'm disappointed in you, Olivia," she said sharply. "I shall be in my study at six o'clock this evening, and unless Fairy G has solved the mystery in the meantime, I will expect you to tell me EXACTLY what has been going on." She gave me a chilly look, and stalked away.

Fairy G waited behind for a moment. "Olivia dear, I know Poppy Room always look after each other, but do try and persuade whoever found the ear trumpet to come and see me as

soon as possible. I'm sure they
meant to return it to Queen
Fabiola, but they really should
have said they'd found it when
Queen Fabiola asked us all at
breakfast." She shook her head.
"I'm afraid it wasn't very sensible
to hide it under Amy's bed.

It doesn't look good. Not good at all." And then she stomped away as well, leaving me breathless. I couldn't believe it! Fairy G actually thought one of us in Poppy Room had found the ear trumpet and hidden it!

By the time I got to the sewing room I felt like pouncing on Diamonde and Gruella and forcing them to confess...but of course I couldn't. Duchess Delia was standing in the middle of the room surrounded by heaps of the most exquisite material, and her assistants were waiting by the tables. The duchess was explaining how we would each have our ideas made up onto a paper pattern, and then – once we'd agreed all the little details – the patterns would be used to make the dresses.

"Please excuse me," I said, and

curtseyed as I came in and slid into a seat next to Jessica.

Duchess Delia waved a pair of scissors at me. "Princess Olivia – where have you been?"

"Erm..." I hesitated. "I found Queen Fabiola's ear trumpet."

If I hadn't already guessed Diamonde and Gruella had hidden the trumpet I'd certainly have known then. They almost jumped out of their seats, and began madly whispering to each other.

"Princesses! If you please!" The duchess waved her scissors again. "Let us continue choosing our material."

Chapter Four

I couldn't help enjoying the rest of the morning, even though I was DYING to talk to my friends. Duchess Delia looked at our drawings very carefully, and listened to all our ideas, and then told the assistants how they should draw the patterns. I chose the most glorious pale violet silk

with flowers embroidered all over
it, and Duchess Delia suggested
I had the sweetest little butterfly
on my sash. It was SO exciting!

By the time the bell went for lunch all the paper patterns were cut out and arranged on the tables, with a little sample of fabric pinned on top of each one.

"By the time you've had your lunch and afternoon free time," the duchess told us, "my assistants will have the dresses pinned and ready for trying on. Please be back here promptly!" She picked up her bag, and swept out of the door.

As we followed, Chloe seized my arm. "Where did you find the ear trumpet?" she asked.

"Was that why you dashed away from breakfast?" Lauren wanted to know, and Georgia added, "However did you know where to look?"

I smiled at my friends, but before I could say anything Diamonde pushed in front of me.

"Can't you guess?" she said loudly. "It was because she found the ear trumpet yesterday, and hid it in Poppy Room!"

"Olivia would NEVER do anything like that!" Amy's eyes opened wide.

Diamonde nodded. "Yes she did. She was trying to get you into trouble."

"That's right." Gruella nodded. "Guess where she put it! Under YOUR bed!"

"So the maids would find it there, and then YOU'D be in trouble!" Diamonde went on.

I stared at her. "That is SO not

true," I said. "I heard a noise in Poppy Room last night, and when I looked out of the door I saw you and Gruella running away. And this morning I suddenly wondered what you'd been doing, and I went to look – and I found the ear trumpet under Amy's bed, and I knew you'd put it there!"

I truly thought Diamonde and Gruella would give in and admit what they'd done, but they didn't. Diamonde turned to my friends. "Did Olivia tell you she'd seen us last night?" she asked.

"No..." Chloe said slowly.

"Did anyone else think they heard noises?"

My friends shook their heads.

"So Olivia's just making it up," Diamonde sneered. "She's trying to wriggle out of admitting what she did."

"That's right!" Gruella nodded. "And typical of Olivia to try and blame it all on US!" And the two of them marched away.

It isn't very often that Amy, Chloe, Georgia, Jessica, Lauren and I can't think of anything to say, but we must have been silent for at least a minute. We were SO shocked!

Then we all began talking at once, and I had to tell the story of what had happened in the night over and over again.

"Are you absolutely certain that you didn't dream hearing the twins coming into our room?" Lauren asked thoughtfully.

Amy took my arm. "Of course she didn't! If she'd dreamt it, how would the ear trumpet have got under my bed?"

"I don't know," Lauren said. "I'm sorry, Olivia. I do believe you, honestly I do – but it does seem a bit weird that you didn't wake us up."

"And none of the rest of heard anything," Georgia agreed.

I saw Chloe and Jessica nod, and my stomach gave a little flip. Surely my friends would believe me, and not the twins?

"Did Fairy G see Diamonde and Gruella?" Amy asked.

I shook my head. "I don't think so. She was coming from the other end of the corridor."

"That seems a bit strange. She saw you, but not the twins..." Lauren scratched her ear. "Oh well." She smiled at me, but I could see she wasn't totally sure I hadn't been dreaming. I felt terrible.

"I don't suppose you could have been sleepwalking, Olivia?" Georgia suggested. "Maybe you found the ear trumpet in your sleep..."

"And you put it under Amy's bed, and because you were sleepwalking that's why you forgot it was there!" Chloe clapped her hands as if she'd solved the mystery.

"But I didn't!" I was beginning to feel desperate.

"I believe Olivia," Amy said firmly, and I was SO grateful I wanted to hug her.

"I've got to get the twins to own up," I said fiercely.

"But how can you?" Amy asked. "We've no way of proving it was them, and not us."

We looked at each other gloomily. She was right.

Chapter Five

The afternoon should have been SO wonderful – but it wasn't. Our dresses were absolutely gorgeous, and Duchess Delia promised that they'd be totally finished by the very next day, but none of us felt as excited as we should have done. It felt as if a black cloud was hanging over us, and I was getting more and more worried about having to see Queen Fabiola at six o'clock. The twins, on the other hand, were more cheerful and pleased with themselves than I'd ever seen them. It was AWFUL!

We were just hanging up our dresses at the end of lessons when Fairy G came bursting into the sewing room.

"I've come to see what you've been doing!" she said cheerfully, and she picked a pink dress off the rail. "This is very pretty! Who does this belong to?"

Over in the corner, Emily put her hand up.

"Lovely!" Fairy G waved her wand. At once tiny flowers blossomed on the pink chiffon. Emily's eyes shone.

"THANK YOU, Fairy G," she breathed.

"A dress for a Perfect Princess!" Fairy G told her, with a beaming smile. Diamonde snorted, but she didn't say anything.

Fairy G picked up another dress, and with a wave of her wand she added sparkles to the sash.

"Ooooh!" Daisy was thrilled.

One by one, Fairy G added a little touch of magic to each dress, until the only ones left were Diamonde's, Gruella's, and the six belonging to Poppy Room. Diamonde and Gruella were positively twitching, they were so eager to see what would happen, but Fairy G suddenly stopped.

"Oh dear," she said. "Perhaps I should have told you earlier? If there's anything you've done that means you're not quite a Perfect Princess, the magic goes the wrong way." She waved her wand over a piece of luscious red velvet, and immediately it turned a nasty drab grey. "Something like that." And she gave all of us in Poppy Room a long thoughtful stare. "Are you quite QUITE certain you want me to go on?"

My friends and I looked at each other, and Amy gave my hand a little squeeze.

"Yes please, Fairy G," I said.

Fairy G turned to Diamonde
and Gruella. "And what do you
two think?"

Diamonde did her best to smile
as if she didn't have a care in
the world, but Gruella rushed to
the clothes rail. She unhooked
her dress, and clutched it to
her chest.

"My dress is very nice as it is, thank you, Fairy G," she said. "I don't want it changed at all."

Diamonde glared at her. "Don't be silly, Gruella!"

"I'm not being silly!" Gruella made a face at her sister. "I'm being careful! And YOU should be too, Diamonde!"

Fairy G raised an eyebrow, but she didn't say anything.

Diamonde swallowed hard, and folded her arms. "Erm...please add some magic to my dress, Fairy G," she said.

Fairy G raised her wand in the air – and Gruella shouted, "Stop!

PLEASE stop, Fairy G!"

But Gruella was too late. Diamonde's wonderful pale yellow dress had turned a disgusting dark mustard colour.

"I TOLD you we shouldn't have taken that stupid ear trumpet!" Gruella wailed. "I just KNEW it would all go wrong in the end! It always does!"

Diamonde didn't answer. She stood very, very still, a strange expression on her face – and I realised she was trying her very hardest not to cry.

"I think," Fairy G said, and she spoke quite gently, "I think, Diamonde, you had better go to your room. Gruella, you too."

We were all very quiet as we watched the twins trail out of the door.

"I don't think Queen Fabiola will need to see you tonight, Olivia," Fairy G told me. "In fact, I have another suggestion. I suggest that we have a rehearsal for the Butterfly Ball, because – as I understand it – Poppy Room are going to float down on a magical carpet of poppy petals. And we don't want anyone falling off. MOST undignified!"

Chapter Six

And that's what we did – and it was SUCH fun! Not one of us fell off, although we did feel nervous to begin with. But by the time of the Butterfly Ball we were experts, and when the magical poppy petal carpet came floating down into the ballroom, surrounded by a cloud of the prettiest butterflies, everybody cheered and cheered and waved – and we waved back.

We even waved to Diamonde and Gruella, who were sitting at the very back of the ballroom...

and I was so happy I had an idea. As soon as the poppy petal carpet landed on the ballroom floor I jumped off and ran to whisper in Fairy G's ear, and she

smiled, and nodded. She waved
her wand, and the butterflies
flittered and fluttered up into the
air and across the room...

and settled on Diamonde's mustard-coloured dress until it was completely covered. She looked down at her dress in amazement – and began to smile.

And when it was time for the butterfly polka I grabbed her hand and made her dance, and Amy twirled and whirled with Gruella.

It was a lovely LOVELY ball...
and I so wanted everyone to
be friends.

Because friends are the very best...don't you agree?

And I'm so lucky that you're my friend too...and the next time we meet, we'll be at Pearl Palace together.

Isn't that just SO exciting?

Win a Tiara Club
Perfect Princess Prize!

There are six tiaras hidden in *Butterfly Ball*,
and each one has a secret word in it
in mirror writing. Find all six words and
re-arrange them to make a special Perfect Princess
sentence, then send it to us. Each month, we will
put the correct entries in a draw and one lucky
reader will receive a magical Perfect Princess Prize!

Send your Perfect Princess sentence, your name
and your address on a postcard to:
THE TIARA CLUB COMPETITION,
*Orchard Books, 338 Euston Road,
London, NW1 3BH*

Australian readers should write to:
*Hachette Children's Books,
Level 17/207 Kent Street, Sydney, NSW 2000.*

*Only one entry per child.
Final draw: June 2008*

Have you read
all the Tiara
Club books?

Welcome to

Tiara Club
The / Club

Join the Rose Room princesses at the Princess Academy!

PRINCESS CHARLOTTE
AND THE **BIRTHDAY BALL**
ISBN 978 1 84362 863 7

PRINCESS KATIE
AND THE **SILVER PONY**
ISBN 978 1 84362 860 6

PRINCESS DAISY
AND THE **DAZZLING DRAGON**
ISBN 978 1 84362 864 4

PRINCESS ALICE
AND THE **MAGICAL MIRROR**
ISBN 978 1 84362 861 3

PRINCESS SOPHIA
AND THE **SPARKLING SURPRISE**
ISBN 978 1 84362 862 0

PRINCESS EMILY
AND THE **BEAUTIFUL FAIRY**
ISBN 978 1 84362 859 0

151

And join

More magical adventures with the Rose Room princesses!

PRINCESS CHARLOTTE
AND THE **ENCHANTED ROSE**
ISBN 978 1 84616 195 7

PRINCESS KATIE
AND THE **DANCING BROOM**
ISBN 978 1 84616 196 4

PRINCESS DAISY
AND THE MAGICAL MERRY-GO-ROUND
ISBN 978 1 84616 197 1

PRINCESS ALICE
AND THE **CRYSTAL SLIPPER**
ISBN 978 1 84616 198 8

PRINCESS SOPHIA
AND THE **PRINCE'S PARTY**
ISBN 978 1 84616 199 5

PRINCESS EMILY
AND THE **WISHING STAR**
ISBN 978 1 84616 200 8

Don't forget

The Tiara Club

at Ruby Mansions

Now make friends with the princesses from Poppy Room!

PRINCESS CHLOE AND THE
PRIMROSE PETTICOATS
ISBN 978 1 84616 290 9

PRINCESS JESSICA
AND THE BEST-FRIEND BRACELET
ISBN 978 1 84616 291 6

PRINCESS GEORGIA
AND THE SHIMMERING PEARL
ISBN 978 1 84616 292 3

PRINCESS OLIVIA
AND THE VELVET CLOAK
ISBN 978 1 84616 293 0

PRINCESS LAUREN
AND THE DIAMOND NECKLACE
ISBN 978 1 84616 294 7

PRINCESS AMY
AND THE GOLDEN COACH
ISBN 978 1 84616 295 4

Also make sure you join

Meet the Lily Room princesses!

PRINCESS HANNAH
AND THE **LITTLE BLACK KITTEN**
ISBN 978 1 84616 498 9

PRINCESS ISABELLA
AND THE **SNOW-WHITE UNICORN**
ISBN 978 1 84616 499 6

PRINCESS LUCY
AND THE **PRECIOUS PUPPY**
ISBN 978 1 84616 500 9

PRINCESS GRACE
AND THE **GOLDEN NIGHTINGALE**
ISBN 978 1 84616 501 6

PRINCESS ELLIE
AND THE **ENCHANTED FAWN**
ISBN 978 1 84616 502 3

PRINCESS SARAH
AND THE **SILVER SWAN**
ISBN 978 1 84616 503 0

*Don't forget to join
the Tiara Club at Christmas time!*

**CHRISTMAS WONDERLAND
ISBN 978 I 84616 296 I**

Two stories in one book

This Christmas, look out for

PRINCESS PARADE
ISBN 978 I 84616 504 7

Two stories in one book

By Vivian French
Illustrated by Sarah Gibb
The Tiara Club

The Tiara Club at Silver Towers

The Tiara Club at Ruby Mansions

All priced at £3.99.
Christmas Wonderland, *Princess Parade* and *Butterfly Ball* are priced at £5.99.
The Tiara Club books are available from all good bookshops, or can be ordered direct
from the publisher: Orchard Books, PO BOX 29, Douglas IM99 1BQ.
Credit card orders please telephone 01624 836000 or fax 01624 837033 or visit our
website: www.wattspub.co.uk or e-mail: bookshop@enterprise.net for details.

To order please quote title, author, ISBN and your full name and address.
Cheques and postal orders should be made payable to 'Bookpost plc.'
Postage and packing is FREE within the UK
(overseas customers should add £2.00 per book).

Prices and availability are subject to change.

Check out

The **Tiara** *Club*

website at:

www.tiaraclub.co.uk

You'll find Perfect Princess games and fun
things to do, as well as news on the Tiara
Club and all your favourite princesses!